DRAGON MASTERS

CHILL OF THE ICE DRAGON

BY

TRACEY WEST

ILLUSTRATED BY

NINA DE POLONIA

SCHOLASTIC INC.

DRAGON MASTERS

Read All the Adventures

TABLE OF CONTENTS

THIS BOOK IS FOR KYLE,

who is as powerful as any dragon I have ever imagined. — TW

Text copyright © 2018 by Tracey West
Interior illustrations copyright © 2018 Scholastic Inc.

Library of Congress Cataloging-in-Publication Data
Names: West, Tracey, 1965- author. De Polonia, Nina, illustrator. West, Tracey, 1965- Dragon Masters.
Title: Chill of the ice dragon / by Tracey West ; illustrated by Nina de Polonia.
Description: First edition. New York, NY: Branches/Scholastic Inc., 2018. Series: Dragon masters; 9
Summary: The Dragon Masters are still reeling from the desertion of Rori and her fire dragon Vulcan, when Mina, a Dragon Master from the far north, arrives with a problem—King Lars needs a fire dragon to defeat the Ice Giant who has frozen his kingdom; and so the Dragon Masters set out to find Rori and convince her to help.
Identifiers: LCCN 2017020251 ISBN 9781338169867 (pbk.) ISBN 9781338169874 (hardcover)
Subjects: LCSH: Dragons—Juvenile fiction. Wizards—Juvenile fiction. Magic—Juvenile fiction. Giants—Juvenile fiction. Adventure stories. CYAC: Dragons—Fiction. Wizards—Fiction. Magic—Fiction. Giants—Fiction. Adventure and adventurers—Fiction. GSAFD: Adventure fiction. LCGFT: Action and adventure fiction.
Classification: LCC PZ7.W51937 Cj 2018 DDC 813.54 [Fic]—dc23 LC record available at https://lccn.loc.gov/2017020251

10 9 8 7 6 5 4 3 2 1   18 19 20 21 22

Printed in the U.S.A.   23
First edition, February 2018
Illustrated by Nina de Polonia
Edited by Katie Carella
Book design by Jessica Meltzer

MINA FROM THE FAR NORTH

My name is Mina, and I need your help."

One of the king's guards had brought the girl down to the Dragon Caves. Drake stared at Mina in surprise. So did the other Dragon Masters — Bo, Ana, and Petra. So did Griffith the wizard.

Nobody said anything at first. Everyone was still in shock. They had just learned that Rori, one of the Dragon Masters, had run away with her Fire Dragon, Vulcan!

So much had happened since yesterday. That is when a Dragon Master named Eko attacked the castle with her Thunder Dragon, Neru. Eko and Neru were captured. King Roland  demanded that Griffith banish Eko. He wanted to keep Neru at the castle.

But Rori thought that taking away Eko's dragon was mean. So she helped Eko escape with Neru, and she and Vulcan left with them.

Then Mina arrived.

Simon the guard coughed. "I'll be going now," he said.

Everyone looked at Mina. She had long, blond hair. She wore a brown tunic and furry boots. An ax was tucked into her belt. And a green stone glittered on a cord around her neck.

"Are you a Dragon Master?" Drake asked. He pointed at the stone. It was a Dragon Stone, just like the one he and the other Dragon Masters wore.

"Yes," she replied. "I am a Dragon Master from the Far North Lands. I train at the fortress of King Lars and Queen Sigrid."

"You must train with the wizard Hulda," Griffith said. "She is very powerful."

Mina nodded. "Yes, but not powerful enough to stop the Ice Giant."

Petra's eyes got wide. "Ice Giant?"

"Vasty is his name," Mina replied. "Many ages ago, he attacked our kingdom with his magic. The kingdom was ruled by a different king then. That king's wizard put a spell on Vasty and trapped him in a tomb of ice. But the giant is awake now, and he wants revenge."

"Why would the Ice Giant try to hurt *this* king?" Ana asked. "He's not the one who trapped Vasty in ice."

Mina's blue eyes looked serious. "All Vasty knows is anger. So he used his magic to turn the fortress into ice. Everyone inside was frozen with it."

"Hulda could not stop him?" Griffith asked.

Mina shook her head. "She tried, but her magic was no match for the Ice Giant's. I tried to stop Vasty with my Ice Dragon, Frost. But Frost's ice powers had no effect on the Ice Giant. I escaped, but Frost didn't." Her voice sounded sad.

"What can we do to help?" Bo asked.

"Hulda once showed me all of you in her gazing ball," Mina said. "I saw your Fire Dragon. Legends say that only a Fire Dragon can defeat an Ice Giant."

Drake looked at the others. *A Fire Dragon?*

"I have bad news," Drake told Mina. "Our Fire Dragon is gone. He and his Dragon Master have run away!"

FINDING RORI

What do you mean, they've run away?" Mina asked. "What kind of Dragon Master leaves her wizard?"

"Her name is Rori," Drake explained. "And, well . . . she doesn't like being told what to do."

Mina folded her arms across her chest. "Do you know where Rori went?"

"She left with a powerful Dragon Master named Eko," Griffith explained. "Eko's Thunder Dragon can create portals that allow Eko to travel far very quickly. Rori and Vulcan could be anywhere."

"So you will not look for them?" Mina asked.

"We were about to discuss that," Griffith replied. "Our king will be angry when he sees that two of his dragons and a Dragon Master are gone."

"Good! Then let's find them!" Mina said.

Griffith shook his head. "It will not be easy. We tried using magic to find Eko once before, and we could not."

Mina frowned. "If you can't help me, I will find some other way to save my people," she said. She started to walk away.

Suddenly, Drake remembered something. "Mina, stop!" he cried. "I think I know where to find them."

Everyone looked at Drake.

"When Diego, Carlos, and I were on an island looking for Eko," he continued, "a thunderstorm hit us. That could have been Eko using Neru's powers to scare us away. We should go back to that island."

"That is an excellent idea, Drake!" Griffith said. "Ana — you and Kepri should go with Drake and Worm. You are Rori's best friend. She may listen to you."

Ana nodded. "Of course," she said. Then she ran to put a saddle on her Sun Dragon.

"Petra and Bo will stay behind with me and Mina," Griffith added. "We will learn more about Ice Giants."

"I am going to the island," Mina said. "This Fire Dragon may be my only hope."

Griffith nodded. "If you insist."

Mina turned to Drake. "How do we get there?" she asked.

Drake put one hand on Worm, his big, brown Earth Dragon.

"Just touch Worm," Drake said.

Ana and Kepri came out of the dragon's cave. Mina touched Worm. Ana put one hand on Worm and one hand on Kepri.

"Good luck!" Bo said.

"Worm, take us to the last island we went to," Drake said.

Worm's body started to glow. Green light filled the room. It got brighter and brighter.

Then Worm, and everyone touching him, disappeared.

ATTACK THEM!

The Dragon Masters, Worm, and Kepri appeared on a green, leafy island. The trees had long, skinny trunks.

"This big, brown Worm brought us here?" Mina asked. Her eyes were wide. "What kind of dragon is he?"

"He is an Earth Dragon. He has amazing mind powers," Drake replied, smiling.

Then they heard a noise.

Rooooaaaaaar.

"That sounds like Eko's Thunder Dragon!" Ana cried. "It came from over there!"

Ana jumped on Kepri and they flew toward the  sound. Drake and Mina ran through the tall trees. Worm swiftly slithered behind them.

They soon reached a group of houses made of tree branches and big leaves. A shield of rippling purple energy surrounded the whole place.

"That looks like Neru's powers!" Drake cried.

"Kepri, do you think your brightest sunlight can break through that energy field?" Ana asked.

A beam of bright sunlight streamed from Kepri's mouth. It hit the purple shield. The energy started to flicker.

Pop! The shield disappeared. Kepri flew forward.

Rooooaaaar! A purple dragon rose up from behind one of the houses. A woman with dark hair rode on his back.

"Eko!" Drake called out. "We are not here for you. We came to talk to Rori."

As he said this, a red-haired girl and her big, red dragon stepped out from behind one of the other houses.

"Rori!" Ana cried happily.

"Rori has nothing to say to you," Eko replied.

Rori's eyes flashed. "Eko, these are my friends. Can't we just talk to them?"

"We can't trust them, Rori," Eko warned. "Neru, attack!"

Neru began to glow with energy. But before the purple dragon could attack, green beams of light shot from Worm's eyes! They zapped Neru, sending him jolting backward.

Whoa! I've never seen Worm do that before! Drake thought.

Eko fell from her dragon's back.

"Rori, make Vulcan attack that dragon!" Eko yelled, jumping to her feet.

Worm's whole body was glowing green now. The green energy surrounded Neru, trapping him.

"They're hurting Neru!" Eko said. "See, Rori? You cannot trust them!"

"Worm is not hurting Nero. And you attacked *us* for no reason!" Drake said. "See, Rori? Eko is the one you shouldn't trust!"

"Rori, do not listen to them," Eko said. "They're just trying to turn you against me. Attack them!"

RORI'S DECISION

Rori put her hands on her hips and looked at Eko.

"Are you going to tell me what to do, just like Griffith?" Rori asked.

Eko's dark eyes flared. "I am nothing like that old wizard!" she said. Then she turned her back to Rori.

Ana ran up to Rori and hugged her. "Please, Rori, come back with us," she pleaded. "We need you and Vulcan to help us save Mina's kingdom."

"Who's Mina?" Rori asked, and then she noticed the new girl. "Did Griffith replace me already?"

"I am Mina, from the Far North Lands," Mina replied. "I traveled to Bracken because my people need the help of a Fire Dragon."

"*Why* do you need Vulcan's help?" Rori asked. "Is this some sort of trick to get me to come back?"

"There is no trick. An Ice Giant named Vasty has frozen our fortress and everyone inside it," Mina answered. "Only a Fire Dragon can defeat him."

Rori frowned, thinking.

"The decision is yours, Rori, and nobody else's," Ana promised.

Rori nodded and turned to Eko. "I am going with my friends. But I will be back."

Eko glared at Rori. She did not say anything.

The other Dragon Masters touched Worm. Ana touched Kepri. Rori and Vulcan walked up and touched both dragons.

Worm let go of Neru.

Then he quickly transported them back to the Training Room in King Roland's castle.

Bo and Petra ran out of the classroom.

"You're back!" Bo said happily.

"Not for long," Rori said. "I am just here to help this girl."

"Mina, from the Far North Lands," Mina said.

Rori rolled her eyes. "Yeah, I got that part."

Petra patted Vulcan's neck. "It's good to see you again, too, Vulcan," she said.

Griffith walked up to them, smiling.

Rori held up one hand. "Don't look so happy," she said. "I'm not staying."

"I hope you will stay, Rori," Griffith said. "I know I was being harder on you than on some

of the others. That is only because I know that you can be one of the best Dragon Masters ever."

Rori looked surprised. "Yeah, um, well, thanks," she said. "But I'm still going back to Eko when this is over."

Mina marched between the two of them. "I am sorry to interrupt your drama," she said, looking at Rori, "but my kingdom needs saving. Are you going to help me, or not?"

TIME FOR A PLAN

I said I was going to help you defeat Vasty," Rori snapped. "Are *you* ordering me around now, too, Mina?"

"Vasty sounds nasty," Bo joked, giving a small smile. Both girls glared at him.

"He is more than just nasty," Mina said. "He is evil. His heart is made of ice."

"Vulcan's flames can melt ice, no problem," Rori said. "My dragon is very powerful."

Mina glared at Rori. "And so is Vasty."

Griffith motioned for the Dragon Masters to follow him into the classroom.

"We will help you, Mina," the wizard said. "But first, we need a plan!"

Griffith pointed to a large map on the table.

"Petra found this map of the Far North Lands," the wizard said. "Mina, can you show us where the fortress is?"

Mina studied the map. She pointed. "Here."

Bo's eyes got wide. "Your kingdom is very far away. How'd you get here without your dragon?"

"I walked," Mina said. "Sometimes I rode on a passing wagon. I took a ship across the water. It took a very long time."

Drake looked at Mina's thick boots. They were caked with dirt from her long walk.

She's brave, Drake thought. *And tough. I don't know if I could have come that far all by myself!*

"We can use Worm to get back to your kingdom quickly," Drake said.

"Good, we must hurry," Mina said.

"We should all bring our dragons," Ana said to Mina. "They can help Vulcan. Shu has water powers. Zera, the four-headed dragon, has poison powers. And you've seen what Kepri can do."

"But Vulcan is the one who gets to melt the giant, right?" Rori asked. Her eyes were shining with excitement.

"Yes," Mina replied. "I just hope your dragon is as strong as you say."

"I can prove it!" Rori said. "Let's go to the caves. I'll ask Vulcan to make a fireball so big..."

"Rori!" Griffith interrupted her. Then he lowered his voice. "You are right. It is a good idea for us to train the dragons today, but we must do it properly. Let's take them outside to the Valley of Clouds."

Rori ran toward the Dragon Caves. She stopped and motioned to Mina.

"Come on!" she said. "I'll show you what Vulcan can do."

CHAPTER 6

BEFORE THE BIG BATTLE

oon they were all outside in the Valley of Clouds — a big, green stretch of land hidden behind the castle. There were mountains on one side, and a forest on the other.

It was the perfect place for training dragons.

"Vulcan, fireball!" Rori cried.

Vulcan flew across the valley. Powerful flames streamed from his mouth. Then they burned out against the blue sky.

In another part of the sky, Ana was flying with Kepri. The white dragon zoomed across the valley like a streak of light.

Down below, Bo's Water Dragon, Shu, was shooting blasts of water at some bushes. They perked up when the water hit them.

Petra was training with her poison dragon, Zera. The hydra was spraying poison mist from each of her four mouths. The mist hit rocks in the mountainside. The rocks slowly started to dissolve!

Drake led Griffith over to Worm.

"On the island, Worm used a new power," he told the wizard. "He shot energy beams from his eyes. They knocked Neru over!"

"Very interesting," Griffith said. Then he pointed at a group of rocks. Blue magic sizzled from his finger.

The rocks floated up one by one, making a tall tower of rocks.

"Worm, can you show me what you did?" Griffith asked.

Worm nodded. He shot green beams from his eyes. *Zap!* They knocked down the tower.

"Excellent!" Griffith cheered.

Rori flew past on Vulcan. "That's nothing! Vulcan could knock down a tower of *big, giant boulders* if he wanted to!" she cried.

After the Dragon Masters finished training, Griffith called to them. "It will be dark soon. Let's go eat," he said. "We will leave for the Far North Lands in the morning."

"Why must we wait?" Mina asked, tapping her boot on the ground.

"If Vasty is as powerful as you say, everyone must be well rested when you face him," Griffith replied. Then he walked off.

Mina turned to Rori. "I think I understand your problem with this wizard," she said, shaking her head.

Rori nodded. "Yeah . . . he's always giving orders."

They all walked back to the castle. Drake stepped next to Rori.

"Thanks for coming back," he said.

She shrugged. "Yeah, well..."

"I know, it's not for good," Drake said. "But I hope you'll stay. We all want you to come back. And I'm sorry if I hurt your feelings before you left."

Rori stopped. She looked at Drake. "Thank you," she said, and she almost smiled.

Then she ran ahead to walk with Ana.

After the Dragon Masters put the dragons in their caves, they ate dinner in the dining room.

Drake could not believe how much Mina ate. She ate almost a whole chicken by herself! Plus potatoes, carrots, bread, and cheese.

She must have been hungry after her long trip, Drake realized. *But she never complained once.*

Then it hit him. Mina was tough. But she and her dragon and wizard couldn't defeat Vasty.

He must be one big, bad Ice Giant! Drake thought.

CHAPTER 7

INSIDE THE
ICE FORTRESS

In the morning, Griffith met the Dragon Masters in the Dragon Caves. He gave them each a warm, furry coat.

"I used magic to make these," he said. "It is cold in the Far North Lands. You will need the extra layer."

Then the Dragon Masters saddled their dragons.

Everyone touched Worm. Rori, Bo, Ana, and Petra kept one hand on their dragons.

"I must stay here to watch over the castle," Griffith said. "Be strong, all of you. Work together and you will not fail."

Drake nodded. "We will," he promised. Then he looked at Worm. "Worm, take us to Mina's fortress in the Far North Lands!"

Drake's stomach flip-flopped as Worm transported them. Suddenly, he felt a blast of cold air on his face.

They had arrived in the Far North Lands. Snow covered the ground as far as they could see.

A glittering fortress rose above them. It looked like it was made of ice!

Rori, Bo, Ana, and Petra climbed onto their dragons.

"The fortress is underneath all that ice," Mina said. "We must melt the ice so we can enter."

Petra shivered. "It's so cold here," she said, holding her hands to her chest.

"Don't worry," Rori said. "Vulcan's about to warm things up. Vulcan, get us inside!"

Vulcan stomped up to the fortress's big front door. *Whoosh!* He shot out a fireball.

The ice melted, revealing a wood door behind it. Vulcan's fire was so hot it burned a hole right through the door!

Rori grinned at Mina. "See how easy that was?" she said. "Vulcan and I can handle your Ice Giant."

The Fire Dragon pushed open the door with his head, and everyone followed Rori and Vulcan inside.

They stepped into a great hall. Drake looked around, his eyes wide. There were people in the room, but they were in blocks of ice. He saw a king and queen on a throne.

A wizard was frozen with her arm raised, like she was about to do magic.

The Dragon Masters climbed off their dragons and walked around, looking at the frozen people.

"Where is the Ice Giant?" Bo asked.

"I do not see him," Mina replied.

"Great! Let's melt everybody and get out of here," Rori said. "Vulcan —"

"No!" Mina yelled. "You cannot melt these people with fire. It could burn them, just like it burned the door."

Rori frowned.

"I think Kepri's sunlight can safely melt the ice," Ana suggested.

Mina nodded. "Yes, try that. Please start with Hulda," she said, pointing to the wizard. "We may need her help to battle Vasty."

Kepri flew over to Hulda and aimed a beam of sunlight at the block of ice surrounding her. The ice slowly began to melt.

Drake looked over at Mina. Her eyes were scanning the fortress.

"It is too quiet," she said. "Vasty must be planning something."

"Maybe he left . . ." Drake suggested.

Rooooooaaaaar!

A dragon swooped down the big staircase in the center of the hall. His shimmering scales had a light blue sheen — *just like ice on a pond*, Drake thought.

"Frost!" Mina yelled.

FROST'S DEEP FREEZE!

Frost ignored Mina. The Ice Dragon opened his mouth and aimed a blast of freezing, sparkling air at Rori and Vulcan.

"Vulcan, stop him!" Rori yelled.

Vulcan charged at Frost, getting ready to hit him with a fireball.

But the freezing air hit Vulcan first. It trapped the Fire Dragon in a block of ice!

"Frost, what are you doing?" Mina yelled at her dragon. "Why won't you listen to me?"

The dragon swung his big head around to face her. Drake noticed a crystal hanging from a chain around the dragon's neck. The crystal gleamed with an eerie blue light.

Mina saw it, too. She turned to the others.

"That crystal is filled with Vasty's magic," she said. "He's controlling Frost!"

"We must get the crystal off him," Bo said. "Shu, blast that crystal off his neck!"

Bo's dragon shot a powerful stream of water at Frost. Before it could reach him, the Ice Dragon hit it with his freezing breath. It turned the water stream into ice.

Then the ice shattered like glass. Pieces scattered across the floor.

Whoosh! Frost aimed another freezing blast at Shu, trapping her in a block of ice.

"Shu, no!" Bo cried.

Petra marched forward. "Everyone, stand back," she said. "Zera, use your poison mist to melt that crystal!"

The hydra aimed all four of her heads at Frost. She shot green poison mist from each mouth. It floated toward Frost.

Frost hit the mist with a freezing blast. Each poison droplet turned into a green snowflake and fell to the floor. Then the blast hit Zera. She was trapped in a block of ice.

"Zera!" Petra yelled.

Drake felt nervous. *Kepri's sunlight powers might work against Frost. But she is busy defrosting the wizard. It's all up to Worm.*

"Worm, can you get the crystal from Frost?" Drake asked.

Worm began to glow green. He closed his eyes. The eerie blue glow in the crystal slowly faded.

The Ice Dragon looked at Mina.

"Worm is using his powers to break the connection that Frost has with the giant!" Drake said.

Mina looked down at her Dragon Stone. It was faintly glowing green.

"Frost! We're connecting!" she cried happily.

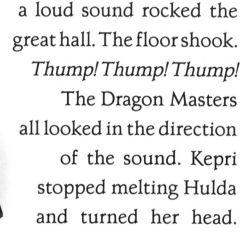

As she ran toward her dragon, a loud sound rocked the great hall. The floor shook. *Thump! Thump! Thump!* The Dragon Masters all looked in the direction of the sound. Kepri stopped melting Hulda and turned her head. A giant — twice as tall as any of the dragons — stomped into the great hall. He had a big, bushy white beard. His eyes glittered like blue jewels. White fur trimmed his clothing and boots. He held a long staff topped with a glowing ice-blue crystal.

Mina pulled out her ax.

"It's Vasty!" she yelled. "Frost, stop him!"

WIZARD VS. GIANT

Who has broken my connection to Frost?" the giant asked in a booming voice.

He saw Worm's glowing green body and frowned. Then he pointed his staff at the crystal around Frost's neck.

An icy streak shot from the blue crystal on the end of his staff. It zapped Frost's crystal.

The glow in Mina's Dragon Stone faded. Now Frost was back under Vasty's control.

Vasty pointed at Worm. "Frost, stop the brown dragon!" he shouted. "I will take care of the attackers."

"We're not attackers!" Mina called up to the giant. "We are here to save my kingdom! The kingdom *you* stole!"

The giant's blue eyes flashed. "Long before humans were here, Ice Giants ruled this land. I am taking back what is mine!"

Frost let out a loud roar. *Rooooooaaar!* He turned on Worm. An icy blast shot from his mouth.

Worm transported! The Ice Dragon's blast hit the floor.

Smart thinking, Worm! Drake thought.

Suddenly, Worm appeared again. This time, he was behind Frost. The Ice Dragon quickly turned to face Worm. Green energy beams shot from Worm's eyes, aimed at the crystal. But Frost was fast. He shot his icy breath at Worm.

Worm swiftly disappeared before the ice-cold breath could hit him.

This made the giant even angrier. Vasty pointed his staff at Drake.

"Your dragon can't save you, tiny human!" he boomed.

"Maybe he can't, but *I* can!" a voice yelled.

Drake gasped as Hulda marched up to Vasty. Kepri had finally unfrozen the wizard! Her blue robes were trimmed with fur. Her white hair was coiled in braids on top of her head.

Hulda held out both arms, and yellow magic shot from her fingertips like lightning bolts. They zapped the giant and he cried out.

Angry, Vasty pointed his staff at Hulda. A blast of magic shot from the crystal. Hulda dodged out of the way as it zoomed toward her.

So much was happening that Drake didn't know where to look. Kepri was trying to defrost Vulcan. Hulda and Vasty hit each other with powerful waves of magic. Frost kept trying to attack Worm, and Worm kept disappearing.

The Ice Dragon began to paw at the floor.

Then Vasty trapped Hulda in a magic beam. She floated right off the floor! It looked like he was about to send her flying across the room.

Hulda's magic isn't powerful enough! We have to help her, Drake thought. *But how?*

Mina ran to Frost. She jumped onto the Ice Dragon's back. He began to thrash. But Mina held on tightly.

"Mina, get down! You'll get hurt!" Drake yelled.

SMASH!

$\mathbf{M}$ ina kept climbing up Frost's back, up to the dragon's neck. She reached for the blue crystal. Frost flew up and thrashed.

Thud! Mina was thrown to the floor. But she got right back on her feet. She jumped back onto Frost.

Drake looked at Frost. The Ice Dragon was trying to throw Mina off again.

"Worm, can you help Mina?" Drake yelled.

Worm's body glowed green as he closed his eyes. The blue glow started to fade from Frost's crystal.

Frost stopped thrashing. Quickly, Mina reached up and yanked the chain off Frost's neck!

Then she jumped off the dragon. She put the crystal on the ground. She raised her ax.

Smash! The crystal shattered into pieces. Vasty's head spun around at the sound. He dropped his magical hold on Hulda. The wizard fell to the floor.

Mina jumped onto Frost's back and patted his neck.

"Good to have you back," she said.

Frost nuzzled his head against her arm.

Vasty stomped toward them. "Get away from my dragon!" he yelled. "An Ice Giant like me is the only fitting master for an Ice Dragon."

Mina's eyes narrowed. "Never!" she cried. "Frost, attack!"

THE POWER OF THE GIANT

Before Frost could make a move, Vasty slammed his big, icy fist on the floor. The whole fortress shook. It knocked Drake off his feet.

Then Hulda spoke. "Vasty, leave this place," she said. "You cannot fight all of us."

The Ice Giant laughed. "Yo! Ho! Ho! You could not defeat me before. You shall not defeat me now!" he said.

He pointed his staff at Hulda.

But Frost zoomed forward, with Mina on his back.

"Frost, now!" Mina cried.

Frost shot his icy breath at the staff, knocking it out of Vasty's hands. Hulda blasted magic from her fingertips. The giant staggered backward.

Worm's eyes closed as his body glowed green. The staff floated up off the floor and then flew into the wall, shattering.

Vasty laughed again. "Yo! Ho! I am still powerful — even without my staff!"

He slammed his fists into the floor, and ice began to spread everywhere.

Worm and Frost went skidding backward. Drake and the others stumbled, trying not to fall down.

Then a loud sound filled the hall.

Roooaaarrr!

Vulcan was free! Kepri had finally finished melting the ice around the Fire Dragon.

Vulcan was angry. He started to wildly shoot flames. Orange fire hit the walls. It hit the ceiling.

"Rori, you've got to control him!" Drake yelled.

Rori ran toward Vulcan. One of his flames almost hit her! But she dodged it and kept running. Then she jumped onto his back.

"Vulcan, focus! We need you to melt that giant!" she yelled.

Vasty spun around. He growled. He clapped his hands together and an ice ball appeared between them.

He hurled the ice ball at Vulcan.

It hit Vulcan. He tumbled backward, but he wasn't frozen.

Only a Fire Dragon can stop Vasty, Drake thought. *That's what Mina had said. But is Vulcan powerful enough to do it alone?*

Drake closed his eyes. He wanted to send a message to Worm — but not out loud. He didn't want Vasty to hear. His Dragon Stone glowed as he thought the words in his head.

Worm, can you use your powers to get Vasty to stop moving?

Worm nodded. His body began to glow.

Vulcan flew toward the giant again. Vasty clapped his hands together, getting ready to blast the dragon once more.

Suddenly, Worm's green energy zapped the giant. Vasty froze in place. He couldn't move.

"Good work, Worm!" Drake cheered.

"Vulcan, now!" Rori cried.

An enormous
fireball shot from
Vulcan's mouth.

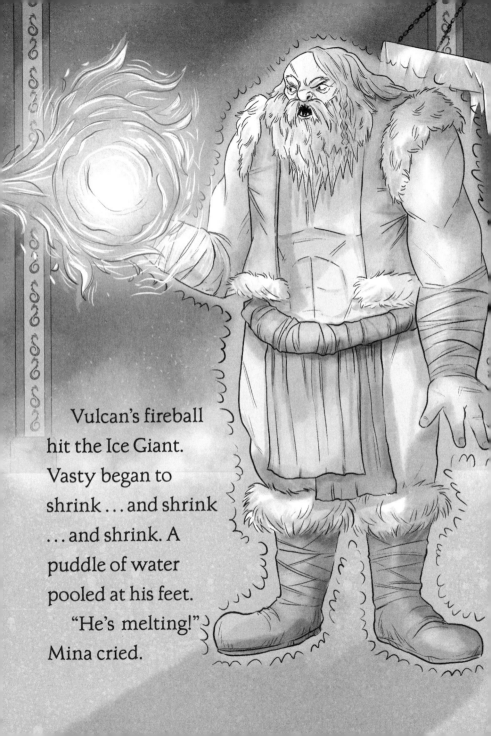

Vulcan's fireball
hit the Ice Giant.
Vasty began to
shrink ... and shrink
... and shrink. A
puddle of water
pooled at his feet.
   "He's melting!"
Mina cried.

Worm broke his hold on Vasty. Now the giant was no taller than Drake's knee.

And he was angry.

"You have not won!" he yelled, but his voice was tiny now. "I will use my magic! I will grow! I will come back larger than before!"

"Thank you for shrinking him, Vulcan," Mina said. "Now, Frost, get rid of this little pipsqueak!"

Frost breathed. A swirling tunnel of ice appeared in the air. The tunnel sucked up the tiny giant.

"Noooooooooo!" Vasty cried.

Then the tunnel disappeared, and so did
the Ice Giant.

FIRE AND ICE

Hulda stood in the center of the great hall. She raised her arms above her head. Yellow magic shot from her fingertips. The ice melted off Shu and Zera. It melted off all the people in the fortress. It melted off the floors and the walls.

The ice did not melt into big, watery puddles. It just disappeared.

The unfrozen people gazed around the hall, confused. Drake thought they looked like people waking from sleep. The king and queen called Hulda over to them.

"My wizard, what has happened?" the king asked. "The Ice Giant — is he gone? And where did all these dragons come from?"

Hulda smiled. "I will let Mina explain," she said. "It was she who rescued us."

Mina bowed. "King Lars. Queen Sigrid. I did not rescue you alone," she began. "These are Dragon Masters from the Kingdom of Bracken. I traveled there to seek their help. Together, we defeated Vasty."

King Lars raised an eyebrow. He reminded Drake of King Roland. But King Lars had a white beard, not a red one. And this king's robes were brown and furry.

"How good of King Roland to send his best Dragon Masters to help me," King Lars said.

Drake looked at his friends. King Roland did not even know they were there!

Rori bowed to King Lars, and said, "King Roland is happy to help you, Your Majesty."

Drake knew this was a lie. *But a smart lie,* he thought.

"I shall not forget this kindness," King Lars said.

Queen Sigrid smiled at them. "Please, stay and let us celebrate this victory with a great feast!"

Bo's stomach rumbled at the word *feast.* But the Dragon Masters knew they couldn't stay.

"That would be very nice, Your Majesty, but we must get back to Bracken right away," Drake said.

King Lars nodded. "Very well."

The Dragon Masters climbed onto their dragons.

Rori turned to Mina. "You were right. Vasty was tough to beat!"

Mina smiled. "And your Vulcan is very powerful. Almost as powerful as Frost."

Drake turned to Mina. "It was nice meeting you," he said.

Mina shook his hand. She squeezed it hard. "I will never forget you," she said.

She looked up at the others on their

dragons. "I will not forget any of you. And if you ever need my help, you will have it."

Drake nodded. "Thank you," he said. He looked at his friends. "Everybody, touch Worm."

The Dragon Masters obeyed. Then Drake touched Worm's neck.

"Worm, take us home!"

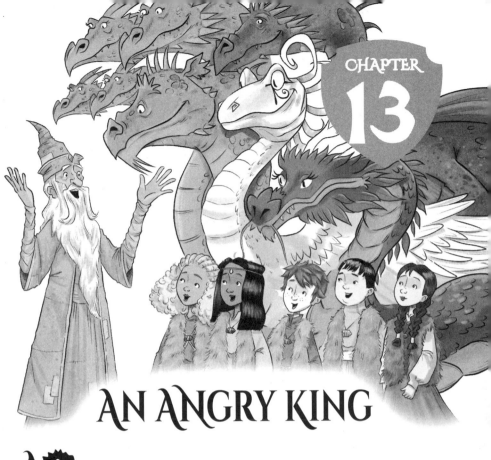

AN ANGRY KING

Moments later, they were all back in the Training Room. Griffith came out of his workshop to greet them.

"You are back! Is everyone all right?" he asked.

"We're all fine," Drake replied.

"Shu and Zera and Vulcan got frozen, but they are better," Bo added.

"And we defeated the Ice Giant!" Rori said. "Vulcan melted him into a teeny tiny giant."

"And then Mina's dragon blasted him into a swirling ice tunnel," Ana said.

Petra nodded. "It was amazing!"

Griffith clapped his hands. "Wonderful!" he said. "You must need to warm up after your adventure. Let's go to the Valley of Clouds."

They spent the afternoon outside in the sunny valley. Griffith used his magic to make a picnic lunch appear. Everyone sat down to eat.

"This is very good," Bo said, munching an apple.

"*All* of this food is good," Rori said, grabbing a chicken leg.

"On the island, Eko only eats fish and weird, pink fruit," Rori added. She shuddered.

Drake looked at Rori. "You don't have to go back there," he said.

"You really don't!" Ana added. "Please say you'll stay."

Rori did not answer right away. Then, just as she opened her mouth, King Roland marched into the valley. Two guards walked behind him.

"Oh no," Rori whispered.

Drake suddenly felt worried. By now, King Roland probably knew that Neru, the Thunder Dragon, was missing. If he found out Rori had helped Eko and Neru escape, he would be very angry.

"Wizard!" the king said in his loud voice.

Griffith stood up.

"I see you have obeyed me and banished the prisoner, Eko," the king continued. "But where is the Thunder Dragon?"

Rori looked down at her lap.

"Your Majesty," Griffith said, bowing. "I am sorry to report that Eko has not been banished. She escaped, and she took her Thunder Dragon with her. It is my fault. I did not use enough magic to keep her here."

King Roland didn't say anything right away. Then his face started to get red. It got redder than his bushy beard. Redder than Vulcan.

"You have failed me for the last time!" he yelled. "I will get a new wizard!"

YOU'RE IT!

Rori stood up. Drake knew what she was going to do. She was going to tell the truth and take the blame to save Griffith.

But Rori didn't have to. At that moment, something fell from the sky and landed at King Roland's feet.

"What is that?" King Roland asked. One of the guards picked up a rolled-up sheet of paper. A circle of melted wax sealed the scroll closed.

The guard handed the paper to King Roland. The king looked at the seal.

"The seal of King Lars?" he said. He unrolled the scroll, then read it out loud.

King Roland,
I must give you thanks for sending your Dragon Masters and dragons to help my kingdom. Your wizard has trained them well. My wizard, Hulda, tells me that Griffith is the finest in the world. Should your kingdom ever need help, my kingdom will be there for you.
                                   —King Lars

King Roland was quiet for a minute. Drake and the Dragon Masters held their breath. *Will King Roland be angry that we went to the Far North Lands without his permission?* Drake worried.

The king spoke slowly. "I'm not sure what you did, Wizard," he said. "But King Lars rules a very large and powerful kingdom. He is a good friend to have. For now, you may remain here."

Griffith smiled as King Roland marched out of the valley.

"Hooray!" Ana cheered.

"But how did that message get here?" Bo asked.

Drake looked up. He saw Frost fly out from behind a cloud, with Mina on his back. Mina waved. Drake and the other Dragon Masters waved back.

Ana looked at Rori. "This has been a good day. The only thing that would make it better is if you would stay."

"Please?" Drake asked.

"Yes, please?" Bo added.

"Please?" asked Petra and Griffith at the same time.

"Well, since you said please..." Rori smiled. "I didn't really like that island anyway. Too hot. And too many yucky fish."

Ana hugged her friend. "Oh, Rori, I'm so
glad you're back!"

Rori frowned. "But I need to tell Eko. It
wouldn't be fair if I just never returned."

"You could write a letter if you'd like,"
Griffith said. "I will use magic to get it to her."

Rori nodded. "Thank you."

"We're not a team without you, Rori," Drake said. "It took all of us to save Mina's kingdom. Who knows what our next big adventure will be?"

"Maybe we will meet more Dragon Masters," Bo said.

"And new dragons," Ana added.

Petra shivered. "I hope we won't meet any more giants."

"Well, I know something we can do until our next adventure," Rori said.

"What's that?" Drake asked.

Rori grinned and touched Drake's arm. "Tag! You're it!"

She ran off. Drake jumped up and chased after her.

Maybe tomorrow, there would be another wizard to battle. Or another kingdom to save.

But not today.